A VICTORIAN MINE DISASTER

A Young Boy's Story

SURVIVORS

A VICTORIAN MINE DISASTER

A Young Boy's Story

Neil Tonge

WAYLAND

Book editor: Katie Orchard
Map illustrator: Peter Bull

This edition published in 2015 by Wayland

Dewey number: 823.9'14 [J]
ISBN: 978 0 7502 9643 4

10 9 8 7 6 5 4 3 2 1

Wayland
An imprint of
Hachette Children's Group
Part of Hodder & Stoughton
Carmelite House
50 Victoria Embankment
London EC4Y 0DZ

An Hachette UK company
www.hachette.co.uk
www.hachettechildrens.co.uk

Every attempt has been made to clear copyright. Should there be any inadvertent omission, please apply to the publisher for rectification. The author and publishers thank the following for permission to reproduce their photographs:

Shutterstock: *cover* Everett Historical

Printed and bound in Great Britain by
Clays Ltd, St Ives plc

Introduction

During the late nineteenth century, coal mining was the key industry in Britain's industrial development. It became the single biggest employer and coal was one of the main exports. Coal was used to smelt iron, to power steam engines, railway trains and steam ships, and to provide gas lighting for streets and the fire in the hearth. Coal lay at the very heart of the Industrial Revolution and the city of Newcastle-upon-Tyne was its capital.

But this prized resource was won from the ground at a terrible cost in human lives. Miners could be swept away in underground floods or blown apart in explosions. In the twelve years from 1845 to 1857 when records of the number of deaths were kept, 12,590 miners were killed. A single explosion in Wallsend pit near Newcastle took the lives of 102 men and boys, while 204 were gassed to death at Hartley Colliery in County Durham.

The desire of the mine owners to make profits drove them to take risks with the lives of their miners. Wallsend pit made over £1,000 a week from the men and boys who worked

12- or 13-hour shifts below ground. The miners themselves earned as little as £1 a week. Even children as young as five were employed as trappers in the pit, opening and shutting doors to ventilate the workings of the mine. The invention of the safety lamps by George Stephenson and Humphrey Davies curiously caused greater risks to be taken in the mining industry. Deeper and more dangerous pits were dug where the gases proved more deadly.

The characters in *A Victorian Mine Disaster: A Young Boy's Story* are fictional, but their lives, experiences and tragedies are typical of many mining communities at the time. The mining disaster described in this story is based on a real explosion that happened at Willington Quay near Newcasde.

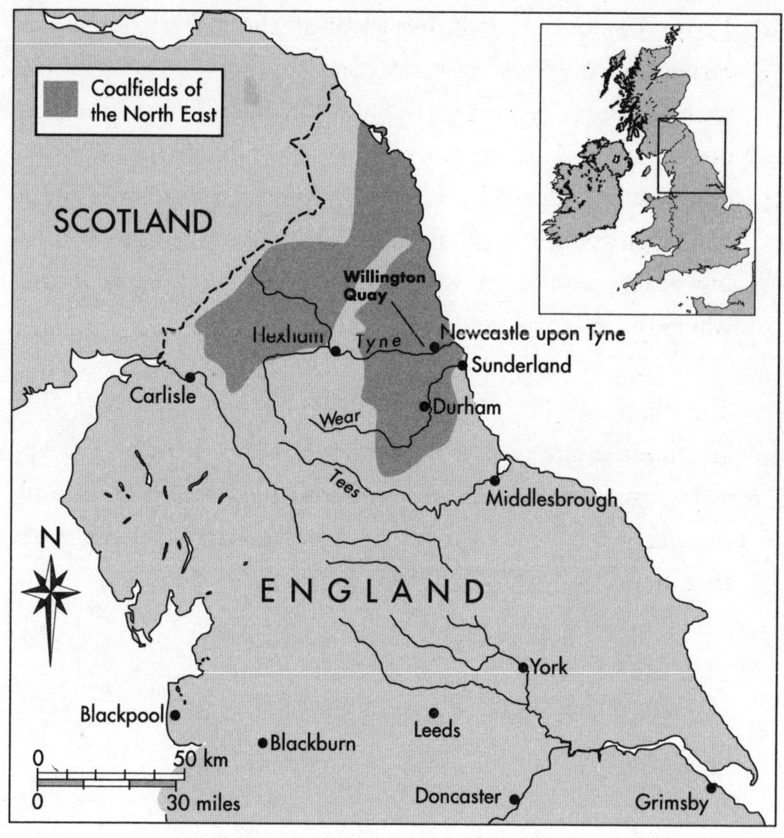

This map shows the main coal-mining areas of the North-East of England in the 1840s.

For Michael Tonge

One

Deeper Than the Worms

'Thomas!'

John Elliot tried to wake his little brother, but Thomas had curled into a tight ball, his hands tucked underneath his cheek.

John ran his fingers through his brother's hair, trying to wake the boy without making him irritable. He hated doing this but he had to. It was time for five-year-old Thomas to join John and his father down the mine. And, although the work was dirty and dangerous, it was a job. What's more it was a job for *all* the men in the family.

'Thomas! *Thomas!* It's time go digging. We're going to dig deeper than the worms,' he said. It was something John's father had said to him when he was Thomas's age, to coax him from his warm bed. That was all of nine years ago, but to John it felt like a lifetime.

John took Thomas by the shoulder and gently shook him. The child's eyes slowly opened as John brought the stump of a lit candle closer to his face. A ball of fuzzy, flickering light fell on Thomas's apple-red cheeks. 'That bloom will soon fade,' thought John to himself.

Turning from his brother, John held the candle aloft. A faint glow spread over the neat interior of the cottage. The kettle hissed and spluttered on the kitchen range from the coals that glowed red beneath. There was little furniture. A table occupied the centre of the room around which his mother, Martha, busied herself 'sawing' slices off the loaf and clattering them on to enamel plates.

John watched his father, Jack, try to rub some life into his left leg. He always said it was worse when the weather was damp and cold. Then the pain felt like a knife probing around inside his knee. Jack had been 'lamed' by a rockfall only two years past. But that was nothing unusual on the Great Northern Coalfield of the 1840s. 'Lamin', as it was called, was common. Many men dragged a useless arm or leg behind them. Others were criss-crossed with blue scars from the coal dust that seeped into their wounds.

John's father bore a scar, too. It was a constant reminder of how accidents could so easily happen in the mines. In 1829 there'd been an explosion. The roof fall had trapped his hand, broken the middle finger and left a scar, shaped like a bolt of lightning. Yet, he'd been lucky. Two other men had been so badly crushed that it had been difficult to lift their remains into the coffins.

At least John's father was alive and able to work. He could still earn good money by wielding a pick as a hewer in a narrow seam. But it was a hard way to earn your living. Water constantly streamed down the walls so that they glistened like ice. Coal dust swirled in the damp and humid air and reached deep inside men's lungs. And the heat below ground was almost unbearable.

John had joined his father underground as soon as he was five. He added to the family's earnings by driving the pit ponies that hauled the coals to the mine-shaft.

And now it was Thomas's turn. It was time he took up work as a trapper, opening and shutting the ventilation doors that circulated fresh air around the mine workings.

John reached down and plucked Thomas from the warm nest of his bed and handed him over to their mother, Martha. She fed Thomas's arms and legs through his clothes as if he were a doll, whilst the boy kept his eyes firmly shut. Martha tried to feed Thomas some porridge but his head slumped forward on the table. He had fallen back into a deep sleep, the food an uneaten lump in his mouth.

Martha handed John and his father their 'bait' – a few crusts of bread and a piece of cheese that was beginning to form a hard rind, tied up in a knotted cloth. Then she passed them canteens of cold tea to quench their thirsts in the overpowering heat of the pit.

Neither John nor his father had the heart to wake Thomas, so Jack hoisted the small bundle on to John's back. Thomas nestled into his brother's collar like a purring kitten as they left the warmth of their cottage and headed into the sharp cold of early morning.

Martha watched them go. As the sneck on the back door clicked shut, she felt the empty quietness of the cottage wrap around her. Jane, her ten-year-old daughter, and the baby would be awake soon enough and the whole row of colliery houses would stir with the rhythm of washing, cleaning and the beating of carpets. But for this brief, still moment in the day, there was a pause, which she filled with the memories of her boys. Now her youngest son was gone. Yesterday Thomas had been a child playing at the door – today he would become a working man.

Two

Underground

In the moonlight, the Elliots joined a small army of silvered shadows who were making their way between the squat rows of colliery cottages towards the pit. Above the pithead, the wheel spun its steel hawsers down the shaft, raising and lowering the 'cages' that took the men to the seams far below ground.

All that could be heard in the stillness of that frosty morning was the hum of the machinery and the slap of the ropes, drawing the men to the pithead as if a spider was spinning its web and they were insects caught in its threads.

Jack strode ahead and handed their metal tags to the underviewer, who would check at the end of the shift that they'd all returned to the surface.

The low murmur of conversation was suddenly broken by a shrill voice.

'What's that, humpback? A sack of coal?'

A finger prodded into Thomas who squirmed on John's back.

John recognized Charlton's voice and gritted his teeth. 'Oh, no,' he thought. 'Not that bully again.' Charlton was always throwing his weight around because his dad was in charge of the shifts. John was getting fed up with being pushed around by the older boy. 'If only things were even between us,' thought John. 'I'd soon wipe that ugly, twisted grin off his face.'

John chose to ignore the snide remark and joined his father in the cage with several other miners. John clenched his fists, desperately trying to control the frustrated rage that burned inside him. Charlton sneered and grinned maliciously, as the metal bar that secured the cage was slammed shut and they began the descent down the shaft.

The brake on the winding engine was released and the cage shot down the shaft like a bullet, the pithead wheel spinning overhead in the grey morning light. Miners pressed close together inside the cage for fear of losing an arm through the open bars, as it hurtled thirty-five metres to the workings below. John had never got used to that dreadful lurch in the pit of his stomach as the cage descended at speed. It always had the same effect on himself and the rest of the men, plunging them into a dark, depressed silence. This was not a deep pit by the standards of the day but it was deeper than any worms would go.

A stomach-turning jolt brought the miners to rest at the bottom of the pit. They spilled out of the cage, then disappeared into the darkness as they sought the narrow seams that radiated outwards from the main gallery. The miners would be confined in these dark tunnels for the next thirteen hours.

Thomas slid down John's back, waking with a jolt when he landed. John gently ruffled his little brother's hair.

Thomas rubbed his eyes, trying to get used to the inky blackness. Ghostly shapes formed before them and then faded into the gloom. Thomas clutched at John's leg as muffled sounds of clanking machinery and voices, distorted in the close and humid air, reached his ears. Thomas looked as if he had suddenly awoken in a strange world where he'd been banished for some dreadful crime.

John felt his father place a hand on his shoulder.

'Take Thomas to the entrance to the seam and show him what he must do,' said Jack. He brushed the hair from Thomas's face, leaving a sooty streak across his brow.

Both boys watched as their father limped off into the blackness then, falling on all fours, crawled into the short seam. Once at the headway, John knew that his father would strip to the waist so that he could work in the steamy heat.

John squeezed his brother's hand tightly and then settled him down on to his haunches whilst he spoke to him. 'Here, Thomas. You must sit here.' John indicated a small, rectangular hole, which had been hollowed in the side of the coal wall of the seam. 'Here's a candle. You keep it lit. When you get used to the darkness, you won't need it. Now, Thomas, you must stay awake. Every time you hear the putters coming with their wagons along the rails, you must pull this rope and open the door for them. Do you understand? Otherwise the door must be kept shut. It's really important. The door keeps out the gas. If the door is left open and the gas builds up, we're all done for.'

Thomas blinked his huge eyes like a forlorn puppy about to be deserted by his master. He didn't want to be left alone in the dark with strange noises wafting in the stale air and with phantoms looming in and out of the blackness.

John sensed his little brother's fears, for he had been just as frightened on his first day in the mine. 'You'll be all right, Thomas. Don't worry. I'll be nearby, harnessing the ponies. I'll call back to you. Da's just along there at the head of the seam.'

John patted his brother's head, turned and walked

away. A black cloud descended on his mind. He didn't want to leave Thomas alone. He'd always been able to keep an eye out for his little brother. He'd held Charlton at bay when the bully had sidled up and threatened Thomas. 'But at least Da won't be far away,' John thought, trying to calm his own fears, 'and I'll be on hand if there's any trouble.'

John glanced back. He could see that Thomas was staring after him, but after a few steps his brother had merged into the blackness that enveloped everything.

Three

Monster in the Mine

Thomas pressed his back deeper into the hollowed niche in the coal wall, scouring the dark for the monsters that must be making the noises he could hear. There was no doubt in Thomas's mind. There was a monster nearby. It was closing in. He could hear the muffled roar of the creature; the grinding of its teeth as it drew closer. He'd already decided that there was no point in running – his legs felt like water and he was trembling uncontrollably. Besides, he could not tell in the pitch-blackness the direction from which the creature was coming.

Terrified, Thomas tried to curl into the smallest ball possible; if he were small and still, perhaps the monster would not see him.

Thomas searched the gloom, peeking out from behind his arm, which covered his face. Would the monster suddenly lurch at him without warning? His bowels ached and he wasn't sure he'd be able to control himself. And then he caught sight of a glint of white. Whether it was the flash of long sharp claws or gleaming savage teeth, he could not tell. He'd only glimpsed it for a few seconds but it was just long enough to know that the creature had found him.

The animal was long and squat and was moving cautiously through the seams as if sniffing out its prey. Then, within several metres of Thomas, the middle of the creature reared up and let out a long, low growl.

'Open!' the monster roared.

Thomas froze.

'Open!' roared the creature, its voice full of fury.

But the little boy could do nothing but whimper. Then the realization of what this monster really was came crashing in on Thomas. 'Oh, no!' he groaned for he could now see the face of the monster, which was twisted in anger, and heading straight for him.

It was Charlton. His eyes were wide with rage, his nostrils flared, and spit drooled from his mouth as he tried to form the words to curse the little trapper. 'I'm going to get you, you little worm! Get that door open! I'm losing time! I'll have to get this bloody heavy wagon moving again!' The words were thrown like daggers at the cringing shape of Thomas, huddled in his cubbyhole.

Thomas pressed his little body deeper into the floor of the seam. The bitter, musty taste of the coal dust spread throughout his mouth. 'Someone help me, please!' he prayed.

But he had little time to think because Charlton was upon him. Grabbing and twisting at Thomas's collar, Charlton hauled him out of his hole and up to his face like a wriggling fish on the end of a line.

Thomas knew he was done for unless he could summon help. Struggling to free himself from Charlton's clenched fist, he yelped at the top of his lungs, 'John! John!' The words did not come out as he had intended. Instead, gulping in a mouthful of air, Thomas's thin, strangled cry for help seemed to melt in the humid air.

Four

Trouble

'There, there! Take it easy. It's John.'

John caressed the pony's neck, smoothed its mane and then pressed his cheek against the animal's muzzle. Singing Hinney gave a gentle whinny as he recognized the familiar touch and smell. It had been John who had named the pony, for the animal's whinny had reminded him of the sizzling, singing sound the oatcake 'hinneys' made as they cooked on his mother's iron skillet at home. Singing Hinney gave another approving whinny as he felt the harness slip over his head.

The pony's pale liquid eyes had long since ceased to be of any use. But his other senses had taken over and he had become sensitive to the different sounds that echoed around his dark world. His sense of smell particularly, was well developed – he would become agitated the moment explosive gases built up in the workings of the mine.

It was over two years since John and Singing Hinney

had first begun to work together and they were now inseparable. If John was not there the pony would move only grudgingly. And although driving the ponies was a task usually given to the older men who could no longer work at the coalface, the ponies worked so well under John that he had been given the job of driver.

John hung the feedbag of oats on a nail at the head of the stall and patted Singing Hinney's head.

'Well, boy, it's time to work,' said John, gently. He led the animal out of the stable and hitched him to the truck. The smaller tubs, filled to the brim with coals from the seams would be tipped into Singing Hinney's waggon. The pony would drag his load to the base of the shaft, where it would be hauled to the surface in the same cage that brought the miners underground.

As John reached the main gallery, he suddenly stopped. He thought he could hear his brother's voice calling out his name. But he could not be sure because the sound was very faint.

'Did you hear that?' John asked Singing Hinney. The animal's ears turned and twitched.

Then John heard his name again. This time he was certain that it was Thomas who was calling out. Leaving Singing Hinney hitched to the truck, John darted along the main gallery and headed for the small side-seam in which Thomas and his father were working. As John turned the corner and ducked into the narrow seam, he saw two struggling shadows. One was much taller and held the smaller shape in its grip.

'Da! John!' The little figure spluttered out his appeal for help.

Seeing John, Charlton threw Thomas to the ground like a limp rag. He stood over his terrified victim with his fists clenched, ready to bring them crashing into Thomas's face.

John filled his lungs and screamed at Charlton, 'Don't you dare, you coward!' John lunged forward, his head lowered like a bull in a charge. Crashing into Charlton, he sent him sprawling across the floor of the seam. As they rolled and hit against the jagged wall, Charlton let out a piercing scream and clutched his shoulder in pain. Roughly, he tossed John aside. A sharp shard of rock caught John on the forehead, making it bleed. But John quickly raised himself into a crouching position and launched himself at the bully. Charlton saw him coming and, kicking out with his feet, hit John hard in the stomach. John was badly winded. He rolled over, gasping for breath.

Charlton staggered to his feet, but, cramped in the small seam, it was difficult for him to re-launch his attack. He quickly searched the gloom for a weapon. Hugging his painful shoulder with his left hand, he snatched a pick from his trolley with his right hand and tried to wield it at John.

'Swine!' Charlton spluttered in frustrated rage. There were tears in his eyes. He was angry, hurt and humiliated, but he was determined to get his revenge. 'I'll finish you Elliots, once and for all. You're scum, sons of a cripple!' He searched for worse to say but, not finding the words, put all his rage into a wild swing with the pick, and aimed at John's head. But the pain in his shoulder, combined with the lowness of the roof, made Charlton mistime his blow. John just had time to roll to one side, before the point of the pick missed his neck by centimetres. Charlton raised the pick again, stumbled, lost his balance and crashed to the floor. The pick struck the coal wall and sent a trail of sparks flying into the fetid air.

The little trail of sparks, like tiny exploding stars in the night sky, was enough to send the world crashing in. During the fight, the trapdoor had remained closed. Odourless and colourless pockets of lethal methane gas – the dreaded 'fire damp' – had begun to seep from the coal, to form invisible, but deadly clouds along the roof of the seam.

In seconds the gas ignited. There was a deafening explosion, followed almost instantaneously by a vicious stream of fire, which raced along the roof of the seam.

Instinctively, John dived to cover his brother from the

blast. Charlton covered his head with his hands and whimpered.

Five

A Narrow Escape

The sound of the scuffle at the entrance to the narrow seam brought Jack Elliot and the other miners running to the scene. They were within metres of the incident when the flash and roar of the fire damp raced toward them, threatening to engulf them in a boiling inferno. Pulling their arms over their heads, they all dived for cover.

Jack, who was in the lead, just managed to shout out a warning, before flinging himself to the ground. 'Fire damp!' he bellowed, before he, too, curled like a baby, wrapping his arms around his head and pulling his legs up into his chest.

One old man, however, was slower to react than the others. Although he was sixty-seven years old, he still worked a full shift at the coalface. The blast caught him full in the face, leaving a raw and bloody mess. He did not even have time to scream. Instead, he clutched his head and groaned as he fell to his knees. He would survive but with the constant reminder of the explosion on his ravaged face.

One of the younger men nimbly jumped to one side in an attempt to avoid the sheet of flames that roared towards him, but in doing so, struck his back against a jagged edge of coal. The shard was as sharp as a dagger and it pierced his back almost to his lungs. He fell on to his knees, gasping for breath.

Fragments of coal flew like a hailstorm, cutting the backs of the miners' hands and naked shoulders. Most escaped severe burns – this time.

Struggling to their feet, the miners quickly checked themselves for injury. Then, half-dazed, they searched for casualties. The air was thick and cloudy with dust and the sickly smell of after damp.

Jack saw the old man first. He bent down on his good knee and cradled the old man's head in his arms. Jack could take little weight on his lame leg and was grateful when his 'marrer', or work-mate, took over. Taking the cork stopper from his canteen, Jack gently poured a trickle of cold tea on the old man's forehead to soothe the burns.

Two other miners in the group bent over the young injured miner who was drawing in each breath with considerable pain. They gently turned him on to his side so they could staunch the flow of blood from the poor man's back. His eyes were wide and uncomprehending, as if to say, 'Why me?' There was no answer, of course, to this question. He had just been in the wrong place at the wrong time.

Although the young man's lungs had not actually been pierced, they had been bruised, and it was likely that a couple of his ribs had been broken, too. He was finished in the pit. If the mine owner took pity on him, he might be given a few shillings to tide him over until he could find a lighter job. But the young miner was now as useless as the mountain of slag that loomed over the village.

Jack was the first to be back on his feet, fearful for the safety of his two sons. He dragged his lame leg behind him, hurrying along the seam as fast as he could to where he had left Thomas. His imagination filled with images of his little boy; cradled in his arms as a baby, being hugged when he fell and grazed his knee. And this morning, too tired to open his eyes. Jack's mind reeled at the injustice of it all. Why did it have to be like this? Why was he bringing children into the world if they were to be killed and injured in the dark bowels of the earth?

Jack knew that there was no point in looking for sense. Children worked and that was that. Nor was there any point in sending them to school – what use were letters to a pitman destined for a life underground? Besides, the more children a miner had, the better a prospect he was. The mine owners would prefer to hire a man who came with his own small army of workers. No, there was no point in searching for answers, but all the same, Jack wished the world were otherwise.

Jack almost collided with Jamie Stephenson, running from the main gallery to the narrow seam. Charlton's father was the underviewer and in charge of the men underground. They both tried to peer through the swirling dust to make sense of the scene before them.

Jack gasped. He could see John lying face down. He was deathly still. Jack closed his eyes, wanting to shut out the agonizing image of his son's unmoving body. As Jack stood paralysed with fear, Thomas's voice struggled to be heard from beneath the body of his brother.

'Da! *Da!*'

Jack glimpsed first a hand and then a face, squirming to be free from under the crumpled body.

'Da, oh, Da, I knew you'd come!' Thomas ran and buried his face in his father's stomach.

Jack hugged the boy tightly, then, scooping him up, rushed to his elder son's side.

'No! Please, God, no!' Sick with fear, Jack turned John over on to his back.

John's eyes were closed.

Jack's heart sank. It was too unbearable. His son was dead. Just as Jack had given up hope, John's eyes flickered open.

Six

An Accusation

John stared, first up into his father's face, then at his surroundings, desperately trying to gain his bearings. He put his hand to his head. There was a deep wound in his forehead and his mind was a swirling confusion of sights and sounds. John could see the relief on his father's face, but, for the moment, he had no clear idea of what had happened.

'Those Elliots! Those damned Elliots! They caused all this!' Charlton had got to his feet. He was screaming at his father and pointing an accusing finger at the three Elliots huddled together.

'That Elliot!' He spat the words out as if they were a nasty taste in his mouth. 'That little runt didn't open the door. I knew the gas was coming and told him to get a move on but he just sat there looking stupid. I was going to open the door myself but then along comes that big lumbering knucklehead, who throws a punch at me. I

knocked him back and so he snatches up that pick to brain me. But he couldn't even manage that – he struck the coal wall instead. It was the sparks. The sparks caused the explosion. He could have killed us all!'

'Hold your tongue, son!' Charlton's father commanded.

'But he could have killed us all . . .' Charlton simmered down and looked humbly at his father as if totally innocent of any wrongdoing.

Jamie turned to John. 'Is this true?' he asked. Even Jamie was never entirely sure when his son was lying or telling the truth.

Charlton was indignant. 'Da! That's what happ—'

Jamie did not allow his son to finish his sentence. He held up his hand for silence. 'John, I'm asking you. Is that what happened?' Jamie waited for a response.

John was confused. He struggled to remember what had happened. There had been an explosion, he remembered that. But he could not work out how it had started. The blast must have blown his brains loose. Yet, deep within he knew that there was something wrong with Charlton's story. It wasn't just that he didn't trust the bully – something else didn't make sense. John could not work out why he was here, not in the stable. He was with his brother. There must be a reason for it but his head was filled with a swirling

black cloud of incomprehension.

'What happened? When . . . ?' John mumbled, but it was no use. He could not collect his thoughts.

Jack rushed to his son's defence. 'Look, Jamie. John's obviously in no state to say anything. Wait till his head clears. One thing is certain – I know my boy, and I'm sure that this is not how it happened.'

Jamie turned to John. 'You're a good man, John, and a good worker, but we cannot be having this. You'll have to see Master Bell when he comes to the office tomorrow. He'll have to decide what is to happen.' Jamie turned to the other miners who had reached the scene and were now standing in a circle. He ordered them to help the injured men to the surface and then to clear away the debris.

Jack was thankful that they were all alive but now it seemed they were finished at this pit. He could only hope that the news would not spread to the other mines. Anyone dismissed from a pit was branded as a troublemaker and it was unlikely that they would find work at the other pits in the neighbourhood.

How would he tell Martha? The mine owned the cottage they lived in – they'd be thrown out if he lost his job.

Jack helped John to his feet and together they slowly

made their way back along the main gallery to the shaft. Supporting his son around the shoulders, he staggered off with the added burden of young Thomas who had clambered on to his father's back. John clung to his father's arm for support.

Jack was convinced that Charlton was lying but it would be difficult to prove whilst John was still dazed.

Seven

Master Bell

Mathew Bell, proud owner of Willington Quay mine, wiped his hand across the dirty office window and peered out at the pithead. The colliery wheel over the shaft was turning, hauling the last shift to the surface.

The mine owner watched as the matchstick figures spilled out of the cage and crossed the colliery yard, their faces covered in grime and grit. Davy lamps swung from the men's belts, clanking against their metal buckles. One or two of the miners exchanged a few words; some even laughed at a joke through mouths that looked like red raw wounds in blackened faces. Young boys trudged wearily alongside them, their eyes blinking in the sudden light. They were like an army of shadows, whose passing through life would be scarcely noticed.

Mathew Bell, a respectable businessman and a pillar of the Church and community, held his chin in his hands as he contemplated the scene before him.

He scratched his chin and grimaced. It wasn't his fault if these people thought that they were hard done by. They didn't have to work for him, after all. And hard work never hurt anyone. He had to work hard himself. He had a heavy burden of responsibility, for it was his job to see to the future; to make sure the coal was won at the cheapest price and sold at the best. These men would have neither work nor houses for their family, if it were left to them.

Lost in his own sense of self-satisfaction, Mathew Bell did not notice in the mass of men and boys that some limped from previous injuries. Nor did he notice the young trappers who clung to their fathers' shoulders, fast asleep on their way home.

The mine owner had much to be proud of. Not only had he pulled himself up by his own bootstraps, through his business as a draper, but he'd bought the lease for the Willington Quay mine and was giving employment to hundreds. He'd earned a reputation for shrewd dealings and had been amongst the first to notice that things weren't going well at the beginning of the 1840s. As a result, he'd laid-off men from work just in time to make sure the business survived those difficult times. When things improved, he would take on more men, but in the meantime it was impossible if he were to make a profit. The winter hadn't been too harsh, so few of the workers he'd laid-off needed to go to the soup kitchens for a free handout of food. It was a pity about the Forster family, though. They'd ended up in the workhouse when the father could find no other work. Still, these things happened. It was God's will. But at least in a Christian country people weren't allowed to starve.

Mathew Bell was convinced that the world was made the way it was and could not be changed. Lost in his own deep thoughts, he did not hear the door of the mine office gently open, nor did he see Jamie Stephenson enter the room.

Jamie gave a discreet little cough to catch the mine owner's attention.

'Ah, Stephenson. What is it, man?' Mathew Bell plucked his gold fob watch from his silk waistcoat, examined the dial and pushed it back into its pocket. 'Time is money,' he declared pompously, puffing out his chest in a display of self-importance.

Jamie held his cap in his hands, his eyes lowered out of respect for the master. 'Sir, I have all the returns for last week,' he said, nervously. 'We're down, sir. There was an accident, an explosion yesterday and it held us up. Two men were—' Jamie's attempt at explanation was cut short by Mathew Bell's interruption.

'Explosion? Careless! The men have the safety lamp. What more is needed?' His voice began to rise in irritability. 'Don't they understand?' he said waving in the general direction of the new shift coming into the yard. 'I give them a livelihood. They *must* fulfil their side of the bargain.'

Jamie chose his words carefully. 'Sir, we did not expect so much fire damp in the pit. We will have to take a little more care to win these seams.'

The mine owner's face coloured with anger. It was as if he were watching piles of silver coins tumbling off a counting table, falling from his grasp. 'Stephenson,' he said. 'You know how much it has cost to sink this shaft. And the engine had to be overhauled at the beginning of the year. None of these things come cheap!' Mathew Bell had invested thousands of pounds to develop the pit, and now he could see his profits begin to disappear. He knew that a ruined businessman had no friends. Everything could be taken from him, including his liberty. Debtors who could not pay were locked up in prison. This could *not* happen to him.

'Sir, there has been an accusation,' Jamie continued. 'A young driver and his brother, a trapper, have been blamed for the explosion.' Jamie told Master Bell Charlton's story of what had happened. 'The driver denies he was at fault and blames his accuser for the accident. There is some doubt, sir, as to the true course of events.'

'Accident! *Accident!* What is happening below ground?

What are you running man? Is it a bear-baiting garden? A bare-knuckle prize fight? Why are we employing common brawlers? You're responsible for the smooth running of this pit! You know that stoppages mean lost profits. Lost profits mean we close down and then everyone loses!' Master Bell could scarcely get the words out for the anger he felt. Losing money hurt him deeply and he need to blame someone for his displeasure. His eyes bulged from their sockets; the veins in his forehead pulsed angrily and his face turned from red to an indignant purple.

'They are outside, sir,' Jamie explained.

'Outside! Why are they still here? Why aren't they gone?' Mathew Bell was bewildered that such villains should still be anywhere near his presence.

Eight

Best Behaviour

On the other side of the door, the Elliots could hear Mathew Bell's rage, but could not make out the actual words. John and his father stood with their heads bowed whilst Thomas cowered between the pair, seeking comfort from their closeness and from the thumb which he was enthusiastically sucking for comfort.

There had been no comfort or joy to be had in the Elliot household the previous evening. Even the baby, Mary, had become fractious and irritable, waking up several times during the night in fits of crying. Not that this disturbed anyone's sleep, since no one could forget the events of the terrible day and the misfortune they feared was to follow.

In bed, Martha had turned her back on Jack and quietly let her tears flow on to the pillow.

Jack had compressed his anger within himself by

clenching his fists, wanting to fight against the injustice of the world. He'd tried to convince himself that all would be well, but deep down in his heart he doubted that it would be so. The master had the whip hand and he'd never been afraid to use it on the back of the working man.

Thomas had done his best to help John remember what had really happened, but the little boy had been so frightened by the incident that even he'd had to block out the bitter memory of the fight and the explosion from his mind.

At last John's head had begun to clear and the fog surrounding the events of the day began to lift slowly. John could now see clearly what had happened and was determined that the truth would come out. In this way, Charlton would get his just deserts and John's own family would be safe in home and work. At least Charlton's father was fair. John felt certain that Jamie would accept the truth. But John knew that he would have to be careful how he explained the whole misadventure. If he dwelt too long on Charlton's part in this, his father may not be so understanding.

The Elliots rose a little later the following morning because they were on a back shift.

Jack was determined that the truth must come out since John had now been able to explain exactly what had happened. 'Jamie's a fair man,' Jack said, trying to reassure his wife. 'Even where Charlton's concerned.'

But Martha feared the worst. 'No man is fair when it's his kin, Jack,' she said flatly. 'Blood is thicker than water.'

It had been a miserable walk to the pit that morning. No one spoke and Thomas trailed behind, holding on to John's hand.

When they arrived at the mine, Jamie had given John no time to explain but had ushered them into the anteroom of the office. They had been told to stand there in silence until the master would see them.

The storm on the other side of Mathew Bell's office door appeared to subside. Then the door slowly opened and Jamie appeared. He signalled to the three Elliots to follow him into the office.

Mathew Bell stood in the centre of the room. His hands were on his hips, pulling back his black frock coat to reveal the gold chain of his fob watch, which hung in a loop across his large stomach.

'Well,' he boomed, 'what's to stop me driving you from this place as the ungrateful wretches you undoubtedly are? I tell you, men, I'd have whipped you from this place, if it had not been for Stephenson here.' He indicated Jamie with a nod of his head. 'Well?' he continued, 'What have you to say for yourselves?'

'Sir, I . . .' Jack began to speak but his words trailed away like wisps of smoke.

John could see his father struggling for the right words. It wasn't right that his father should have to speak for him. John desperately wanted justice to be done, but it was time for him to speak for himself. He stepped forward. 'Sir,' he began uncertainly, 'my father is guilty of nothing. If there is to be blame, let it rest upon my head. It's true that I got into a fight with Mr Stephenson's son, Charlton, but he was about to strike my little brother. I could not stand by and let that happen. It was the first day that Thomas had been down the pit and because everything was strange to him, he was slow at his duties. Sir, this will not happen again. But if you must punish anyone, punish me!'

The master grunted and narrowed his eyes.

Jamie stepped in quickly, grateful that John had not gone into the detail of the story, and had played down Charlton's part in the disaster. 'Sir, may I suggest that they be put on probation,' he said. 'That way I can keep an eye on them. One more incident and they will be dismissed.'

John and Jamie's pleas seemed to calm Mathew Bell. But he still wanted to demonstrate that he had the power to do with them as he chose – and he wouldn't hesitate to use it.

'Very well, then,' he declared. 'But if there is a whiff,

just a *whiff* of further trouble, then you'll wish you'd never been born. Now, get this rabble out of my sight, Stephenson.' He wrinkled his nose and with a wave of his hand he ushered them from the room like an unpleasant smell.

Closing the door of the office, Jack turned to Jamie. 'Thank you, Jamie. I won't forget this.' He held out his hand to shake, but Jamie held back.

'You're hanging by a thread here,' he muttered. 'I can't . . . won't protect you if there is a next time.'

'There won't be a next time,' Jack said firmly, trying to reassure him.

The Elliots closed the door behind them and descended the stairs leading into the colliery courtyard. Charlton was standing at the bottom of the staircase watching them, his face twisted in a malicious grin, his arms folded over his chest, looking triumphant. He knew he'd won this battle.

'Pay no heed!' John's father warned. 'We have been put on our best behaviour.'

Jamie followed the three Elliots outside. He frowned at his son, who had wiped the smile off his face and was staring skyward with an expression of unconcerned innocence.

John boiled with anger. He wanted to get even with Charlton but not at the expense of his family. Above all, he wanted life to be fair and it wasn't, not for folk like him.

Nine

A Time to Reflect

Charlton had kept up the pressure on John in the days that followed the accident. He was always careful not to be caught by his father, but whenever he got the chance he would shoot a sly, gloating glance in John's direction.

A week after the fight, Charlton deliberately chose a place in the cage facing John. He said nothing but grinned all the way on their rapid descent down the shaft, goading him to lash out. John glared back but clenched his fists by his side to control his overwhelming desire to hit the other boy.

John's father had noticed the silent stares of hatred between the two boys and moved forward to cut the bully from John's view. Jack placed his left hand on his son's shoulder and squeezed hard. His lightning bolt scar glowed red with the pressure.

John knew that his father was reminding him of their bargain not to cause trouble and forced himself to relax.

'This is so hard,' John thought. 'But I have no choice. Our livelihood is at risk if I allow Charlton to make me angry.'

As John parted from his father and Thomas at the stable entrance, his father looked back at him. He smiled through pressed lips and nodded his head as if he knew that John would not let him down.

John watched as his father and little brother faded into the darkness with the other miners. Charlton was the last to pass the two Elliots and as he did so he cast a backward glance at John, grinned and made a shaking gesture with his right hand as if he had caught a rat and was shaking the life out of it. His intention was clear. He would take it out on Thomas given half a chance. And then Charlton, too, melted into the gloom.

Reaching the entrance to the narrow seam, Jack crouched in front of Thomas. Taking him by the shoulders, Jack explained that he must stay alert, not only for the putters' sake but also to keep the fresh air moving through the pit. Lighting Thomas's candle, Jack patted his son on the head and told him not to be afraid. Then he scrambled on all fours to the head of the seam.

Thomas gripped the candle as hard as he could, believing that the guttering light itself would ward off any spirits and monsters that the dark and his imagination could conjure up. As he sat in his hollowed refuge he gradually distinguished the steady tap of the picks from the other sounds around him. His father wielded one of those picks and, he reasoned, as long as that reassuring noise reached him he would be safe.

As John hitched Singing Hinney to the coal truck, he could not dismiss the events of the last week from his mind. He must stay out of trouble at all costs, for his family's sake. But his mind could not put aside his sense of unfairness, and as he tightened the harness around the pit pony, he was unusually harsh. Singing Hinney bristled.

'Sorry, Hinney. I didn't mean to take it out on you,' he said, patting the pony's mane.

The flickering candlelight cast eerie shadows in the galleries where the other men worked. John wondered if they felt the same way as he did. After all, there was time to think down here.

Looking at his fellow miners, John saw himself and the others as little better than convicts, prisoners of the mine, digging their way out to light and freedom. He wondered if there really was a way out. Out of the mines altogether . . . No. There was no way out! Not for the likes of an uneducated boy such as himself and his mates.

John's thoughts turned back to his father and Thomas. If Charlton was determined to make life for his family difficult, how could he stop him? How could he protect them? John felt close to despair. He could not, and would not be bullied and nor would he let his family suffer, either. He poured out his feelings in gentle whispers to Singing Hinney.

The pony snickered at each pause as if it knew that John was troubled. 'I know. I know,' the blind pony appeared to be saying.

'What am I to do?' wondered John. 'I cannot bear to let Charlton get away with it any longer.'

Singing Hinney shook his head as if he could understand every word.

Smiling to himself, John took a handful of Hinney's mane and tugged playfully at it. 'Of course! You understand everything!' he said to the pony. 'I have no choice but to guard my temper.'

Ten

Explosion

Enclosed in the confines of the seams and mine workings each miner had the freedom to think and imagine better times, whilst they toiled endlessly.

One miner, Joseph Armstrong, imagined himself above ground, gazing at the midday sun through the fluttering wings of the pigeons he kept for racing. Next to him, his marrer, Elias Crozier, quietly repeated the letters of the alphabet, which he was struggling to learn at the Sunday school. Close by, another miner, whose wife had recently given birth to a daughter, saw his new baby's face glowing in the candlelight. But most of the men tortured themselves with the imaginary taste of the longest glass of beer in the bar.

For Joseph Armstrong and Elias Crozier, these were to be their last thoughts. The dark world in which they worked and imagined better times, suddenly heaved as the fire damp exploded and ripped through the workings of the mine. They had no chance – it was their candle that had ignited a dense pocket of deadly gas, that hung above them like a noose on the gallows. Little trace remained of these poor souls but red streaks upon the coal.

Barely a second passed between this first explosion and the ignition of other pockets of fire damp throughout the pit. The earth quivered, sending shock waves far and wide. Stout timber props supporting the roof were blown out and torn apart like splintered matchsticks. Unsupported solid walls of stone crumbled and fell, crushing the men beneath. The earth twisted and stuck the cage fast in the mineshaft like a cork in a bottle.

Below ground it was like a battlefield. Thirty-five miners were either dead or dying. Those that survived the explosion were still in grave danger, having to fight for breath as they suffocated in the after damp.

At the bottom of the shaft, two trolley drivers, just turned fifteen, were clinging to life. They were scarcely recognizable – the explosion had so severely burnt them that their clothes had fused with their bodies.

At arm's length from the trolley drivers, two miners lay curled and blackened from the terrible scorching heat. An ugly splinter of wood, a metre long, lay deep in one of the men's chests, a fragment from one of the props that had been blasted apart. A horse and pony lay nearby, both mangled and badly burnt.

Several metres beyond the dead animals, the roof had collapsed, cutting off all those beyond. Several men had died in the great crush of stones. Near the stables, the coal had caught fire and dense clouds of smoke were billowing along the gallery, burning the small pockets of oxygen that fed the flames but upon which survivors would depend for their lives.

Three men who had been working in the face of the west drift had been shaken but were unharmed by the explosion. They ran towards the main gallery to make their escape, but the after damp was so thick that they stumbled and could not breathe. One man had stuffed his nightcap into his mouth in a vain attempt to stop the poisoned air reaching his lungs, but it was no good and he collapsed. The other two men stumbled a few paces further on before crumpling to the ground and dying for want of air.

During the explosion, John was blown against the wall, but had been protected from the full effects of the blast by Singing Hinney, who had sagged and almost fallen on top of him. As he gasped for air, John tried to push himself to his feet with his hands, but the coal shaken loose by the blast made it difficult for him to stand upright. Singing Hinney appeared through a swirl of dust and debris. The pony hooked his head under John's shoulder, helping him to his feet. John was badly winded and grasped hold of the pony's mane to steady himself.

The front of the stable was on fire and the flames were licking up the sides of the stalls in which two ponies lay dead and dreadfully burnt. A third pony reared, wild-eyed and with its mane ablaze before it went crashing through the bar in front of the stall. Then, in a maddened frenzy, it raced off down the main gallery.

'Oh, God!' The words broke from John's lips as he surveyed the destruction all around him. 'Thomas! Da! What has become of them?' John had to find them, and quickly. Time was running out fast – the after damp was seeping through the pit.

Eleven

Gonners

You shall have a fishy
On a little dishy
You shall have a fishy
When the boat comes in.

Dance to your Daddy
Sing to your Mammy
Dance to your Daddy
To your Mammy sing.

Martha sang gently to her baby as she rocked its cradle. Jack had made the baby's crib in which little Mary lay from old timber from the mine. He'd spent weeks working on it before Mary was born.

The birth had not been easy, as Mary had tried to come out backside first and the women of the village had needed to run to fetch the surgeon at the mine to help with the delivery. The families paid into a club at six pennies a week for the doctor's services, but if he was called out in an emergency, more money had to be paid. This always hit families hard. Since that day, Mary had been a fretful child, as if she'd not forgotten her uneasy passage into the world.

Martha's soothing voice wooed the crying baby to sleep, allowing Martha to get on with the washing. Martha was proud of her little cottage and kept it clean, despite the grime from the pit that seemed to settle everywhere.

She looked around the room with satisfaction. Everything was in its place and an air of contentment hung everywhere. Two china dogs stood guard on the mantelpiece. Jack had won them at the huge fair that came to the Town Moor in July every year, and Martha had happily carried them home. Now, they had pride of place over the hearth where the whole family gathered in the evening. The kettle stood hissing on the hob and the evening meal was already prepared and ready for the oven. Jack and the boys would be hungry, ravenously hungry, after working the numbing thirteen-hour shift.

When they'd left on the morning of their interview with Master Bell, it was as if a funeral had taken place. Jack had gripped his wife by the shoulders and told her not to worry; they'd be all right. And, although having the whole family put on probation was a strain, Martha was grateful that they'd lost neither jobs nor home.

She thought back to the day when Jack had had his accident. Some of his work mates had came to the door and taken Martha down to the mine. She remembered seeing Jack's face, visibly white despite the sweat and coal dust that covered him. He told her then not to worry and told her yet again when the surgeon had set his leg badly, leaving him with a permanent limp.

'Well,' she thought, 'we've survived hard times before.'

Martha shook her head. Her life was too busy to waste time thinking about such things. And today was the busiest day of all – washing day.

'Jane!' she called to her eldest daughter. 'Come on, pet. The copper's boiling in the outhouse. Bring the sheets!' Martha disappeared through clouds of steam into the little brick shed that housed her copper tub in which all the washing was done. It was bubbling like a witch's cauldron. Jane appeared carrying a huge armful of sheets, her small pinched face peering over the top of the pile.

The sheets were bundled into the copper pot and Martha kneaded them with her wooden poss-stick, squeezing out the dirt.

'Jane! Keep an eye on things here,' instructed Martha as she rushed back into the cottage to complete the dusting. She'd barely crossed the threshold when the floor and walls shook, followed by a deep rumbling sound. The china dogs tottered towards the edge of the mantelpiece, hovered for a moment and then plunged to the stone flags below, shattering into tiny pieces.

Martha squeezed her eyes shut and muttered, 'Oh, God!' She knew in an instant what this meant – the pit had been blown apart. Three of her family were below ground . . .

Martha grabbed a shawl from the back of the scullery door and swathed her head and shoulders in it. Jane was at the washhouse door, her eyes wide and startled.

'Come on, Jane! Leave the washing!' shouted Martha.

Scooping up baby Mary, Martha and Jane left by the back door and joined the stream of shawled women and children that was flowing like a torrent of muddy water to the pithead. They were silent, all anxious to discover if their families were safe.

Fearfully, the women poured into the colliery yard where a dense cloud of smoke hung over the pithead. A burnt acrid smell stung the nose and throat. It was clear that the explosion below had been devastating. The women began to form into small family groups. Occasionally, one of the women would break away from their group and join another to enquire about their menfolk. The women's sense of belonging together was forged by tragedies such as this. A brutal life was always better when troubles were shared.

The yard was a bustle of activity. Jamie was barking out instructions as men rushed to and fro. Fences were torn down and stretchers improvised. Davy lamps, tools and ropes were brought out from the mine storeroom.

Before Jamie and the rescue party could descend the mine, the mangled cage had to be released. Two lines of men took the strain on the ropes, which had been secured to the twisted metal. The men pulled as hard as they could. Their muscles strained to breaking point. They groaned and gritted their teeth, putting all their strength into clearing the blockage. All were aware that time was running out and this was the over-riding thought that spurred on all their efforts. It took an anxious half-hour before the twisted metal was dragged, screeching and clattering over the courtyard. Then Jamie and the rest of the rescue party were ready to climb aboard the replacement cage and descend into the mine shaft.

Once at the bottom of the shaft, it was some minutes before the rescue party became accustomed to the horrible gloom. They could hear groans from some of the miners. But they were not prepared for the tragic sights that met their eyes.

The first victims they found were two lads, both of them trolley drivers, but they survived only a very short time after their discovery. Lying close to them were two other lads who were both dead. The rescue party made little headway to the west of the pit. The timber supports had been blown away, bringing the roof crashing in to block the rest of the gallery. Near these falls of stone a horse and pony were found, both severely burnt and mangled. Worse, the air was thick with after damp and the men in the rescue party were beginning to feel sick and giddy themselves.

Twelve

Singing Hinney

John knew there would be a rescue attempt. But he also knew it would take some time to organize. For the moment the whereabouts and safety of his father and younger brother were uppermost in his mind and he had to act quickly.

'Da, Thomas! We've got to find them, Hinney.' John could hardly form the words, which came out between choking coughs. The after damp was creeping its poisonous way into his lungs and he knew he must protect himself. Tearing the shirt from his back, John soaked the material in Singing Hinney's trough of water. Next he ripped the garment in two, tying one piece around the pony's muzzle and the other around his own mouth. This would help, but only a little.

Ominously, the flames at the entrance to the stable were beginning to die out. This meant that there was little air left to feed them. The explosion had blown out all lighting, and as the fire died John was plunged into the unseeing world of his pony. To Singing Hinney, the lack of light made no difference. He had learnt to use taste, smell and hearing to find his way around his black world.

'Hinney! You must find Da and Thomas,' gasped John.

The pony threw back its head and gave a whinny. John held on desperately to the pony's back, trusting absolutely in the animal. Hinney plodded out of the stables and into the main gallery. John knew that he had to find his family, no matter how difficult this might be.

The pony plodded slowly, picking its way carefully through the debris. After several precious minutes had passed, Singing Hinney stopped and began to scratch at the ground with a hoof. John guessed he'd been brought to the entrance of the narrow seam, marked by a small mound of rubble. This was where Thomas would have been sitting.

'Are we here? Is this it?' he asked the pony, fearfully. Singing Hinney stayed rooted to the spot, nodding his head gently.

'Thomas! Are you there?' John called out as best he could in the choking atmosphere.

For a moment there was silence. Then, from the folds of blackness there emerged a whimper, followed by a second cry and finally a reply. 'John! Help me!'

John's heart felt a surge of joy and relief. Thomas was alive!

John clawed at the small pile of stones he could feel in the pitch black, whilst little rivers of dust streamed from the weakened roof above, threatening to bury him under a second fall. John felt a small hand reach out for his and then Thomas's little face appeared at a hole in the rubble. Grasping both of his brother's hands, John pulled Thomas through the gap and hugged him tightly. Tearing a strip from the moistened shirt around his mouth John tied it to Thomas's mouth.

Thomas's cubby-hole in the coal wall had saved him during the roof fall but what of their father?

'Thomas, where's Da?' John knew he needed to be quick if he were to save them from suffocation.

Thomas shook his head. 'Dunno, John. Dunno.'

'Thomas, we need your candle and matches. Can you go back through the gap and fetch them?' John could feel his brother shrink into him.

'Go on. Don't be afraid,' he said. 'We need them to find Da.'

At the mention of their father, Thomas disappeared through the gap. A few moments later, he scurried back. He passed the candle and matches to John. The match flared into life and John lit the candle, but there was so little air left that it barely flickered and almost went out . . .

Thirteen

A Suspicious Gentleman

One by one, bodies were brought out slowly from the pithead. Wives and daughters tried desperately to stifle their cries and dab tears from their eyes. As the remains of their loved ones were identified, some women let out howls of utter despair. Women whose husbands and sons had not yet appeared gulped in relief before waves of anxiety returned once more.

Martha watched each sad procession with dreadful anticipation. Some of the bundles were tiny – was her Thomas wrapped in one of the shrouds? Like the other women, she tried to get as close to the stretchers as she could, to learn the dreadful truth as soon as possible. 'No one can have survived,' she thought to herself. The longer they waited, the less chance there was that her family would be brought out alive. Martha's heart ached.

Few noticed or took any interest in a smartly dressed gentleman who stood at the colliery gates. His deep-set eyes surveyed the dismal scene. He rested his hand upon a silver-topped walking stick, one foot crossed in front of the other. Then, he took a small notebook from his inside pocket, licked the lead of a pencil and started to make notes.

The gentleman stayed by the gate for some time, keeping close to the shadows cast by the pillars upon which the gates were hung. It was as if he did not want to attract attention to himself. Completing his notes, he snapped the book closed, placed it in his inside pocket and made for the little group now on the edge of the crowd of women.

'Ma'am, forgive me for intruding at this difficult time,' he said, raising his top hat and bending his head in a short bow.

Martha looked into his strong face, then scanned his well dressed appearance. She was instantly and deeply suspicious. 'Who is he?' she thought. 'Certainly not one of us,' she concluded.

Everything about the man was different, from the way he dressed to the way he spoke. His polished words told of a life of privilege far removed from Martha's own. And his hands – they'd never seen a day's hard work. He belonged to the master's world, not her own.

Martha did not speak, afraid that she might say something that might be held against her. But then, not to answer a gentleman might bring trouble, too.

John Roby Liefchild had met this distrust before. When he'd first arrived in the North-East, he could not understand the Geordie dialect of these people. He'd had to study carefully as if he'd been learning a foreign language, before he felt confident enough to talk to them.

Stricken by the death toll in the pits, particularly amongst children, the government had sent inspectors such as Liefchild to find out all they could about conditions in the mines.

'Ma'am, I understand your distress,' Liefchild tried to reassure Martha. 'May I speak with you? I have been charged with investigating terrible disasters such as this in order that the government may address the problem.'

Martha wondered how this man could possibly understand what she was going through. And what did the government care for their problems? 'Are you one of the master's men?' she enquired, timidly.

'No, ma'am.'

'Sir, my husband and two of my children may be lost to this world. I can think of nought else right now.' Martha did not want to be distracted from the safety of her family. Whatever this strange man wanted – it would have to wait.

'Of course, ma'am. Forgive me. I will intrude no longer. May God protect you and your family. I will call when decency permits.' Liefchild made a short bow, brushed the brim of his top hat with his hand, turned on his heel and left Martha and her girls to their despair.

Fourteen

The Rescue

John poked the candle stump through the gap that led to the narrow seam. His eyes gradually adjusted to the feeble light that flickered and sent shadows dancing against the gallery walls.

'Stay here, Thomas,' said John. 'I won't be long and you'll be safe here until I return.'

Thomas clung to John's arm. 'I won't stay in the dark, John. I want to find Da, too!'

John could see that his little brother was frightened, but he was too conscious of the dangers to risk Thomas's life any further. 'This is what we will do, Thomas. We'll make this hole a little wider so I can slide through. You will stay in your little hollow. You'll be safe there and I won't be far away. All right, Thomas? Will you be brave?'

Thomas nodded and John turned to widen the gap in the fallen stones. It took another minute before John felt it was safe enough to wriggle through. Thomas held on to John's ankle and was hauled through to the other side of the roof fall, desperately afraid that he might be left behind.

The air was a little fresher on the other side of the fall but the after damp would soon seep through. John pressed his little brother into the niche and reassured him that he would not be long. Then John set off up the narrow gallery, his hand shielding the flickering flame. He could hear and feel the dust and grit falling from the shattered roof and an occasional creak of the timber pit props warned him that they were straining under the immense weight of stone above.

John had not gone far when he made out the shape of an overturned trolley, which had come off the tracks and was tilted on its side. Beneath the overturned wagon, he could just distinguish the shape of a miner, held fast by the coal which had tumbled from the tub.

Could it be his father? Hurrying to the side of the track, John put the candle on a large slab of coal and scooped the loose coal aside with his arms until he'd uncovered enough to be able to turn the body. John hooked his arm under the miner's shoulder and lifted him, hoping against hope that it would be his father and that he would be alive.

John reached back for the candle and, plucking it from

its perch, held it near the miner's face.

It was too much to bear. It was not his father. It was the person he hated most in the world – Charlton!

For a moment, John was tempted to hit that hated face with a rock. 'Who would know?' he reasoned. His left hand began to tighten its grip on large stone nearby almost without him realizing it. But, as he did so, Charlton groaned and his eyes opened.

'You!' The word was squeezed out of Charlton's mouth in hatred, which quickly turned to snivelling pleading. 'You've got to help me, Elliot.' But even in his desperate situation, Charlton could only think of getting his own way by bullying and issuing threats. 'If you don't help me, my da will see you from the pit,' he snarled.

'You can't demand anything from me!' shouted John. He looked down on his enemy who for once was completely in his power. What was he to do? Could he leave him?

But despite his contempt for Charlton, John could not cause him harm. Putting his shoulder behind the tilted tub, John forced it to the other side of the heap of coals which had emptied on to the track.

Charlton wriggled free, but when he attempted to take the weight on his right leg, he fell with a scream to the ground.

'Keep still!' John ordered and felt around Charlton's

ankle. It was swollen, but he could feel no bones sticking out, either through the flesh or near the surface.

'I don't think your leg's broken,' said John. 'You'll make it but I can't get you out yet. First I must find out what's happened to my da. I'll be back.' John got back to his feet and set off down the seam. The sounds of Charlton's whimperings faded away into the dark.

John got little further, as a vast fall of stones blocked the way. Tears of desperation ran down his face as he scanned the blockage with his candle, hoping that he could find a way through. But it was hopeless. The stones were huge and densely packed. John stood silent for a moment, wondering whether he should fling himself at the barrier before him and force his way through. But he knew that such an attempt would be pointless.

As John stared at the rocks, he noticed that one stone looked slightly odd. Then, as he looked closer, he realized that he was not staring at a rock. It was a hand. He fell to his knees and wiped away the dirt from it until he could feel the flesh beneath his own fingers.

A scar, like a bolt of lightening ran across the back of the hand from the wrist to the middle finger. John stared at it for a moment. He had found his father but he was too late. John's head crumpled toward his father's hand, already turning cold as the blood drained away. He pressed his father's hand to his burning cheek. It was the hand that had held his when he was a child; one of the hands that had tossed him into the air and caught him as he chuckled and laughed with delight as a little boy when they had walked the heaps together on a Sunday afternoon.

Now, his father was dead. John's father had finally been destroyed by the cruel life of the mine.

John would have stayed there for ever if it had not been for his little brother, whom he must now get to safety. Charlton, too, he would also have to help. Why Charlton could not have been swept away instead of his father, John would never understand. But he knew that things happened, not because they were fair but because they just happened. All you could hope for was a little luck and a lot of mercy. John brushed the tears from his eyes and staggered back to Charlton, black hatred in his heart at the injustice he had encountered that day.

'I knew you'd come back. You had to, Elliot,' sneered Charlton. He had lifted himself up on to his elbows and was still full of threats.

'Shut up!' John spat the command out in disgust at the coward that lay on the ground. He dragged the bully to his feet, deriving a bitter satisfaction from the squeal that came from Charlton's lips as he tried to put weight on his injured foot. Slinging Charlton's arm around his shoulders, John half-carried, half-dragged the boy along the gallery to where Thomas was waiting for him.

Thomas scrambled out to meet them as soon as he saw the dim candlelight draw closer, expecting to find John with his father.

John unhooked Charlton's arm from around his shoulder and let him drop to the ground. Charlton winced but made no protest.

'Where's Da, John?' asked Thomas, quietly.

For a moment John was not sure what to say. He did not want to admit the truth, but there seemed no point in denying what had happened. 'Da was killed, Thomas. The roof fell in on him. He died quickly, Thomas.' John spoke slowly and clearly, keeping a tight rein on his emotions. He did not want to break down and cry. Not at this moment. He had to be strong for Thomas's sake, and he had to stay in control. He needed to gear everything now to getting Thomas to safety.

Thomas said nothing but a tear sprang into the corner of his eye and ran down his plump cheek.

It was unbearable. John knew that Thomas understood. He would not see his father again and all that would be left of him would be pictures in his head. But John could not linger here. He had to stir them all to action. 'Right, we must get moving,' John burst out. 'It's unsafe to stay here any longer.' There wasn't time to mourn his father now. Now was the time to get his brother and the ungrateful Charlton to safety.

Thomas went through the gap first, followed by Charlton, who protested as John pushed him from behind. The bully's swollen foot dislodged a stone as he scrambled through the gap, which, in turn, brought two or three more crashing behind him, nearly trapping John's hand in the fall.

John wasted no time in following Charlton. He could see that the great stone slabs above, which had been held in place by smaller stones, were now beginning to slide forward to seal the gap. He'd barely made it through when he heard the rocks come crashing down. A cloud of choking dust billowed through the hole.

Once clear of the fall, John lifted Charlton under the shoulders, propped him against Singing Hinney and then pushed him on to the pony's back. Singing Hinney shuddered and tried to shake himself free of the unwelcome burden, until John said a few soothing words in his ear. John grasped the pony's reins with one hand, whilst holding the candle in the other. Thomas held on to Singing Hinney's tail and the boys set off down the main gallery. But the air was thick as soup with after damp. Each breath had to be fought for. They would not be able to survive for long.

* * *

Meanwhile the rescue party, equipped with safety lamps, was making its way along the main gallery. They had found no one alive so far and hope was fading.

John was exhausted and beginning to stagger as the after damp reached deep into his lungs, making his head swim. He called out to Thomas to hold on tight but he wasn't sure whether his brother had heard him or even if he was still there.

John fell to his knees, his hands sinking forward into the flinty floor of the gallery. He couldn't go on. His brain began to tell him that it was easier just to lie down on the ground, curl up and go to sleep.

Then, Singing Hinney whinnied loudly. John's head jerked upward. In the distance he thought he could see small blobs of light like fireflies, dancing in the inky darkness.

'Hallooo! Halloo! Is anyone there?'

The sounds swam like fish in and out of John's mind. His head bowed again. All he wanted to do was to fall on his side and drift away into oblivion. Somewhere deep inside, he heard his father's voice, rousing him as he had done every workday morning for the last nine years. He could see his father's face swim into the gloom before him but the image quivered and trembled as if it was under water.

'C'mon, John! Time to go. The worms is digging and so must we.'

John smiled to himself. Da said that all the time.

And then his father's voice became more irritable as it could be on a winter's morning when all John wanted to do was snuggle deeper under the blankets. *'John! I can't wait here all day! We've got work to do!'*

'Yes, Da, I'm coming.' John staggered to his feet. Calling weakly at first but growing in strength, he shouted down the gallery, 'Over here, Da! Here we are! Thomas and me!'

The bobbing lights began to dance as the rescue party broke into a run. John knew little about what happened next for he began to lose consciousness. One of the miners picked up Thomas and carried him in his arms. Two others supported John, whilst Jamie Stephenson proudly took Singing Hinney's reins and led him along the gallery to the mine-shaft, overjoyed that his son was still alive.

Fifteen

Hope

Above ground, Martha was rapidly giving up hope. Twenty bodies had been recovered so far – all dead from the blast or from suffocation in the after damp that had followed the explosion. As the minutes and then the hours passed, it became increasingly likely that her own family had not survived. Perhaps they would never be discovered? Perhaps they would remain buried under hundreds of tonnes of rock until they, too, became fossils like the coal itself . . .

The wheel on top of the mine-shaft began to spin as the cage was brought to the surface yet again.

Martha pressed forward, clutching Mary in her arms, whilst Jane tugged at her mother's shawl. The cage reached the surface and was full of the men from the rescue party. Martha craned to see beyond them. With a clank, the bar over the cage was thrown back and the men emptied on to the platform. Each sad arrival had plunged her deeper into a sense of hopelessness. There seemed less and less possibility of her men surviving.

Martha's heart was racing. Two of the miners were supporting a figure; one held a child in his arms. The child, the child, looked like . . . it was . . . *it was* . . . it was Thomas and, thank God, there, between two of the miners was John. Her sons were safe! But . . . but where was Jack?

Martha rushed to her boys, kissing Thomas all over his sooty cheeks and hugging John, with the baby still pressed to her bosom. She could not stop thanking God for their safe return, whilst tears of relief flowed down her cheeks.

Jamie came to their side and took both of John's hands in his own. 'Thank you, John, for saving my son. I don't know what I would have done without him. I will do anything to help you and your family. Anything.'

John did not know what to say in reply. His father was dead. No one could help him with that. And now he was going to have to tell his mother. It was hard enough finding the words to tell Thomas, but this was unbearable. How could he break his mother's heart?

Martha looked at John with eyes wide in anticipation.

Wearily, John began to explain. 'Ma . . . Da . . . I'm afraid, Ma, that . . .' His words trailed away for he could see by the look of emptiness in his mother's eyes that she already understood.

'I know, John. I know,' she said calmly, hugging him tightly to her.

The Elliots left the colliery yard. They were a sorrowful group. John put his arm around his mother's shoulders. They passed grey-shawled women, faces glistening with tears. Others pressed their hands to their faces, deep in grief as the men's bodies were laid out in two rows in the colliery shed awaiting the surgeon, who would pronounce on their manner of death. Then they could be made ready for burial.

It took until late in the evening before all the bodies were recovered. In a matter of seconds whole families had been devastated. Thirty-five miners, many of them boys and young men, had been killed.

Only three had survived.

Sixteen

Something Must Be Done

After the children were put to bed, John and his mother stayed up all night, staring into the hearth of the kitchen range. The coals glowed red and as they burned, forming miniature caves from which yellow lights shone. Pennants of smoke trailed up the chimney released from little pockets of gas within the coal, spluttering and running in tiny streams of bubbling tar. So much warmth for so much misery.

They remained in this state of limbo until the morning sky was streaked with grey and a thin, watery sun tinged the clouds with crimson. There would be no work today. It was time to bury the dead. Then the debris from the mine had to be cleared.

John watched his mother fill the kettle from the pump outside in the street, which she then placed on the hob for it to sing. Even death could not stop all the routines of the household.

Martha was already busy. There was so much to be done. The baby needed to be fed and changed. Jane needed to be roused from her bed to help with the chores. Clean clothes needed to be ironed, needed to be ready . . . for the funeral. The thought sent a shudder through Martha's body. There was no man beside her; no man to wash and clean for; no man to share the happiness and the worries.

A sharp knock at the door made them both start from their thoughts. They resented the disturbance, both wanting to be left to deal with their grief. John glanced quickly at his mother before unhitching the sneck and opening the door.

A tall gentleman stood before him. He took off his top hat and held it by the brim along with his gloves and walking cane. 'May I offer my condolences to your family,' he said. 'I have just learnt of your tragic loss.'

John was startled and began to stutter a response, 'My mother . . . She's . . . not well, and . . .'

'I met your dear mother yesterday and I wish to offer my sincere regrets for your loss. May I come in?' the man continued.

'Who is it, John? Is it about the funeral?' John's mother joined him on the step, opening the door wider so that she could see who had come knocking. It was John Roby Liefchild.

'Forgive me, Mrs Elliot, for this intrusion. If you could spare me a few moments, I trust that some good can come out of your terrible loss.' Liefchild seemed genuinely concerned.

Martha ushered him to a seat, apologizing all the while for the poverty of their surroundings, whilst Liefchild assured her that he had not seen such a well kept cottage in all his travels.

John was resentful at first. This gentleman seemed no different from the bosses that had sent his father down the pit to his death. 'Are you . . . are you with Master Bell?' John loaded the question with contempt.

'No. I have been sent by the government. There are concerns, young man . . . deep concerns regarding the great loss of life in the coalfields. Concerns over the employment of young children in such circumstances, making them vulnerable to death and injury,' said Liefchild in the same way that John had heard the preacher thunder at in his Sunday sermons.

Liefchild coughed and then changed to a softer tone. 'Do forgive me but I would like to ask your family about the nature of their work in the mine.'

Martha hesitated. They were in a very vulnerable position. The master had control of both cottage and pit. Offend him and they could all be turned out, with only John as the breadwinner of the family. 'Well, sir, I'm not sure. I have just lost my . . .' Martha gave John a long, meaningful look to hint that he should be careful in his choice of words.

But John could bear it no longer. He was sick of the unfairness, sick of the pain and anguish caused by the terrible conditions in the mine. And now his father was dead. Well, he would not stand by and watch his little brother suffer the same way. All the anger and resentment at the manner of his father's death poured from him like a breached dam. 'I will tell all, Ma!' he said, boiling. 'I *will* tell all!'

There had been no holding John back. He had explained that he'd been barely five himself when he'd first been employed in the mine and now Thomas was doing the same. He described how his own grandfather had been drowned when the mine had flooded; how his father had been 'lamed' and now killed, and how the bosses said there was 'nought' they could do about it for this was in the nature of mining. John was determined that things must change. He wasn't sure how, but change they must. Only that would make sense of his father's death and the deaths of the others.

After an hour in the Elliot household, the government inspector snapped shut his notebook and thanked them for their frankness.

As Liefchild left the Elliot's cottage, John touched the

gentleman's arm and said in slow and deliberate tones, 'Sir, something must be done!'

Liefchild nodded to John. Yes, something must be done. The sorrow and sincerity he had found in the little cottage amongst all that tragedy had touched Liefchild deeply. All workmen had the right to refuse their labour but children, well, that was a different matter. Children were too young to decide and ought to be protected by the law. But Liefchild knew that even if they banned young children working in the mine not all parents or employers would agree with it. 'Ah well,' he concluded as he walked away, 'that's for others to decide.'

Historical Notes

The government did produce a report on child employment in the coal mines, and a public outcry followed its publication. Illustrations showed children harnessed to tubs of coal as if they were animals; they showed naked men and boys hewing and putting coal. Most heart-rending were the pictures of the trappers, boys as young as five and six sitting in the darkness, opening the ventilation doors on which the entire safety of the pit depended. It seemed not only cruel, but dangerous to trust the safety of the pit to such young children.

In 1842 the Mines Act was passed, which forbade the employment of women and girls and all children under the age of ten in underground working. Inspectors were appointed to make sure the law was obeyed.

The new law was bitterly opposed by the great coal-owners of the region. Lord Londonderry, who led the campaign against the new law, warned inspectors that they would certainly be assisted in going down the pits but could expect no help in coming back up. His threat was clear. The mine owners would not co-operate.

But the tide of feeling was against his lordship and the other mine owners. The plight of the trappers in particular swayed public opinion. Bad as their working conditions were, it had taken Liefchild a while to realize that when a child said they had been 'sore tired' they meant that they'd collapsed with fatigue and that a 'hurt arm' frequently meant a fracture.

Improvements, however, were slow in coming. Even Liefchild admitted that he had never actually been down a pit, explaining that, 'Everyone was hostile to such a search. Two persons who attempted it, nearly lost their lives.' The law was widely ignored. Small boys were still employed as trappers in the ten years that followed and if an owner was ever taken to court, which was rare, he could expect a fine of less than ten pounds – a trifling amount for a rich mine owner.

Explosions and deaths continued and public opinion demanded even tighter controls. By 1850 the law was made tougher; by 1860 anyone under twelve was forbidden employment in the mines and the hours worked were reduced to ten. By the end of the nineteenth century, safety and employment had improved considerably. It was a battle, however, that was won at a terrible cost in death and injury.

Further Information

If you would like to find out more about Victorian Britain, these books will help:

Bingham, Jane, *Explore! Victorians* (Wayland , 2015)
Goodwin, Jane, *All About: The Victorians* (Wayland, 2015)
Hepplewhite, Peter, Men, *Women and Children in Victorian Times* (Wayland, 2015)

More information about the conditions in Victorian mines and personal accounts from miners in the 1840s can be found on this website:

mylearning.org/coal-mining-and-the-victorians/p-2070

The Parliamentary Commission Reports of the time also give fascinating glimpses of child labour.

Glossary

After damp Choking gas created after an explosion of methane gas.

Back shift The night shift.

Colliery A mine.

Davy lamp A safety lamp invented by Humphrey Davy for detecting gas in the pit.

Driver Loaded the wagons hauled by the pit ponies.

Fire damp Explosive methane gas.

Hewer A miner who worked at the coal face.

Hawsers Steel ropes that hauled the cage up and down the pit.

Poss-stick Large wooden stick for pressing the dirt out of clothes.

Putters The boys who loaded coal into the wagons.

Seams Deposits of bands of coal.

Trapper A small boy who opened and closed ventilation doors to make sure fresh air circulated around the mine.

Underviewer The foreman of the mine. He was responsible for checking that every miner who went down the mine shaft returned safely at the end of each shift.

Other titles in the Survivors series:

9780750296359

9780750296366

9780750296427

9780750296434

9780750296298

9780750296304